FUN WITH DRONES

Coloring And Activity Book

Fun With Drones

Coloring And Activity Book

First Edition
ISBN 13: 978-1-948-251-01-3
ISBN 10: 1-948251-01-9

Designed & written by: Sharon Rossmark and Wendy Erikson
Illustrations by: Camille Tinio

http://womenanddrones.com/
Twitter: @WomenAndDrones

About the Authors

Sharon Rossmark is an American entrepreneur, mentor, presenter, and advocate for STEM/STEAM education. She is also the founder of WomenAndDrones.com the premier global platform featuring women who are disrupting, innovating and shaping the future of the drone industry. Sharon is a FAA certified drone pilot.

Wendy Erikson is a television journalist and mother of three girls who discovered drones through her interest in photography. After realizing the value of drones as an educational tool, she made it her mission to share this exciting way of introducing children to the world of robotics, aeronautics and aviation. Wendy is a FAA certified drone pilot

We are a global organization with a mission to support, connect and inspire women who work or enjoy a hobby in the growing drone industry.

Women And Drones is also dedicated to promoting STEM/STEAM education for children through the wonder of flying robots!

Learn more about Women And Drones and our educational products by visiting: http://womenanddrones.com/

Why Teach Children About Drones?

Drones are an exciting subject for students, teachers and parents, not to mention an ideal pathway for STEM/STEAM.

The learning process presents many educational opportunities, from introducing the fundamentals of flight to exploring the real world applications for this technology.

Drones are being used for studying whales, documenting disasters and delivering medical supplies to remote parts of the world. The possibilities for future applications are endless. Teaching curious youngsters about drones now can lead to some important uses down the road.

About This Book

What's a drone? How can drones help people? Can flying drones be my job when I grow up?

These are questions this activity book answers as we introduce children to the basic vocabulary, safe practices and concepts that are important for operating drones. From coloring and counting drones to word puzzles and mazes, we want to make learning about drones fun!

You and your child will see many girls along with boys, pictured in this book. This is a purposeful, important part of our commitment to engaging more girls in science, technology, engineering and math careers. This introduction to drones can be an interesting and exciting learning experience for the whole family.

Dedicated to the next
generation of
STEM and STEAM
Innovators

Why Are Drones Called Drones?

It sounds silly but the word drone was first used a long time ago to describe a bee! In a busy bee hive the drone bee was known for being a little lazy and not doing as much work as the other bees. Years later the military started building small flying machines that did not have a pilot on board. They were flown by someone on the ground using a remote control.

Whether it's because the machines needed help to fly (and that seemed lazy) or maybe because they made a buzzing sound like a bee, someone started calling them drones.

Smart Drone Flying Tips

- Use a safety checklist
- Never fly at night
- Fly below 400 feet
- Fly so you can see your drone with your eyes
- Never fly near other aircraft
- Never fly near emergency responders
- Never fly near an airport
- Respect the property of others – Do not fly over people's property without permission
- Always check the weather conditions before you go out to fly a drone

A Few Words You Should Know

Aerial: Drones can be used for "aerial photography" which means taking photos of things on the ground while flying in the air.

Battery: A battery provides the power for the drone so it can fly.

Data: Another word for the photos and other information drones can collect while flying.

Drones: Flying robots.

Hobby or recreational use: Flying your drone for fun or amusement.

Line-of-sight: While flying your drone you must to be able to see it at all times using only your natural vision (which includes glasses and contacts, but not binoculars).

Pilot: The person flying a drone.

Safety Checklist: A list of important steps to take before every drone flight.

UAS: Unmanned Aerial System – Another name for a drone, including the remote control and communication system between them.

UAV: Unmanned Aerial Vehicle – Another name for a drone!

Parts of the Drone

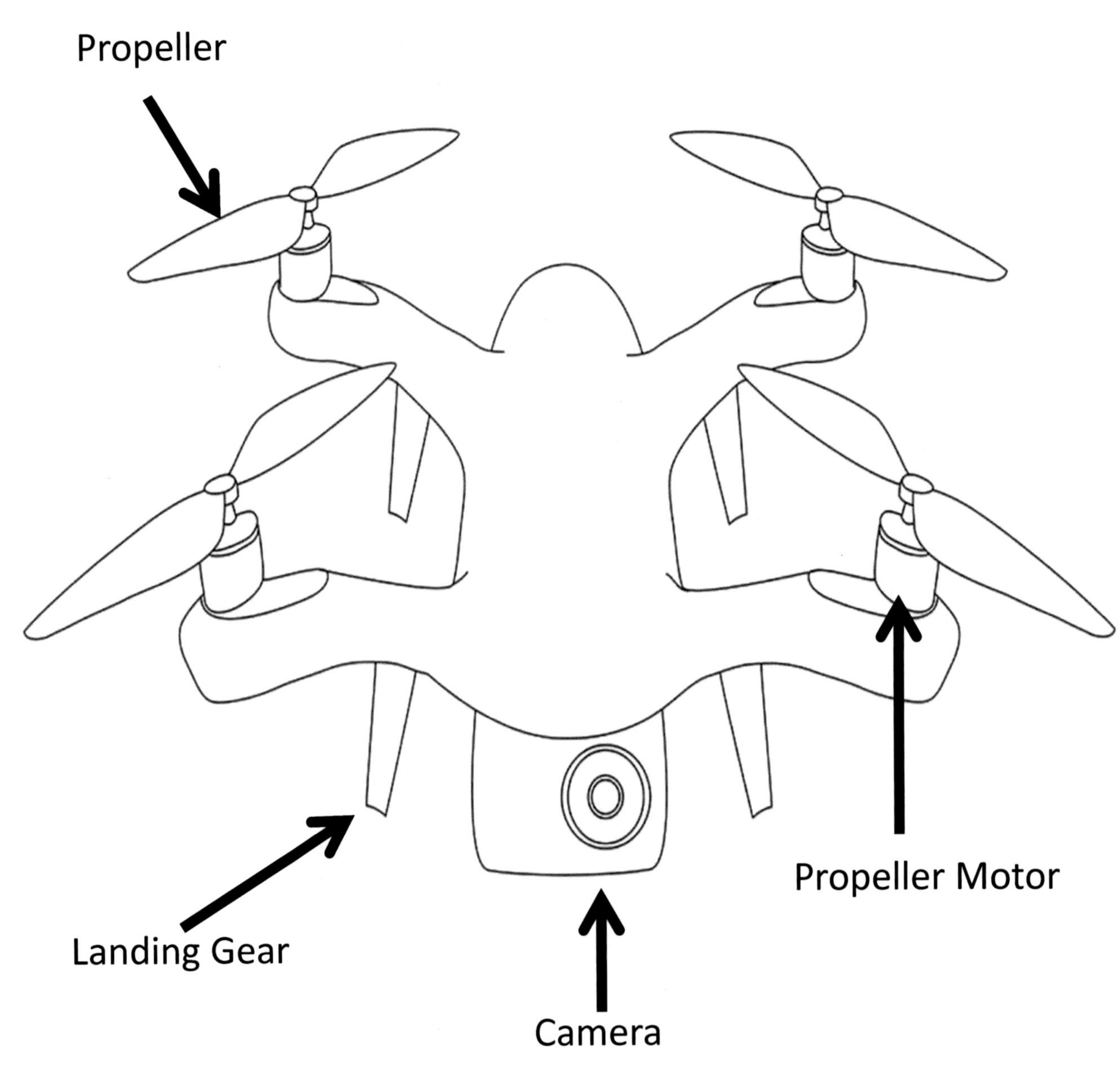

The best way to improve your drone flying skills is with practice.

Some people fly drones to take photographs and videos from the air.

Safe flying is fun flying.

What's the difference?

What's the difference?

©2018 W&D

Be a good neighbor, do not fly over people's property without permission.

Safe flying means always making sure you can see your drone with your eyes.

Criss Cross Puzzle

Write the word for each clue in the grid.

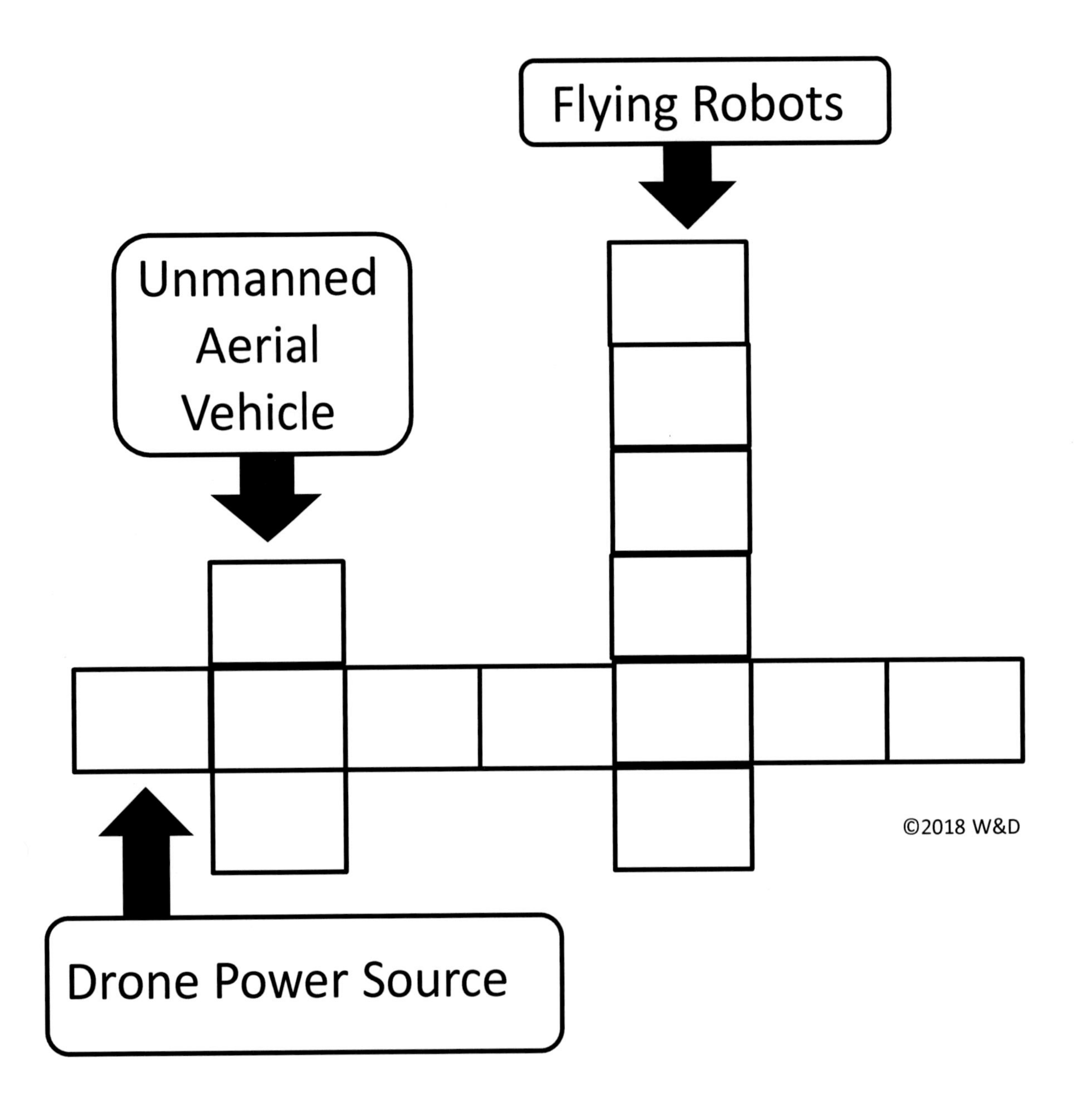

People who race wear special goggles to help them see where their drone is going.

LEARN ABOUT DRONES

1. Paying attention to the rules when flying drones is important:

S __F __T Y

2. A flying robot is called a:

__RO__E

3. Someone who controls the flight of an aircraft including a drone:

P__LO__

4. Since drones do not have people inside them, they are called:

UNM_NNED

Help Leah read the clues and fill in the blanks.

EXPERT DRONE
SERVICE
BUILD A
DRONE
WORKSHOP
SATURDAY
9:00 AM

Drone Maze

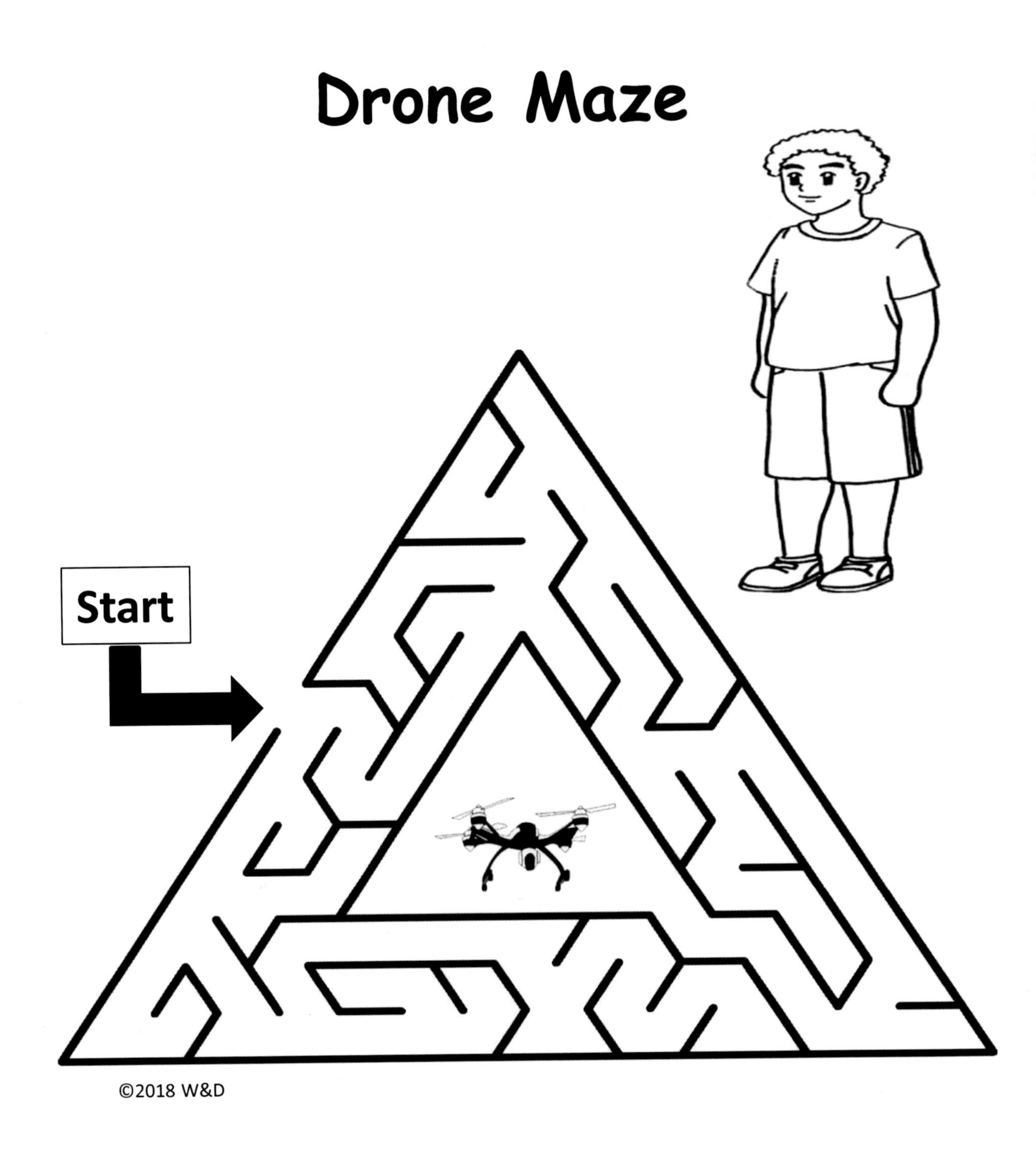

Show Liam the flight path to find his drone.

Maryam is practicing to be a professional drone photographer some day.

The Drone Zone

What's the difference?

DRONES

Count the drones.
How many drones are in the sky?

What's wrong with the way Sophia is flying her drone?

Drone Maze

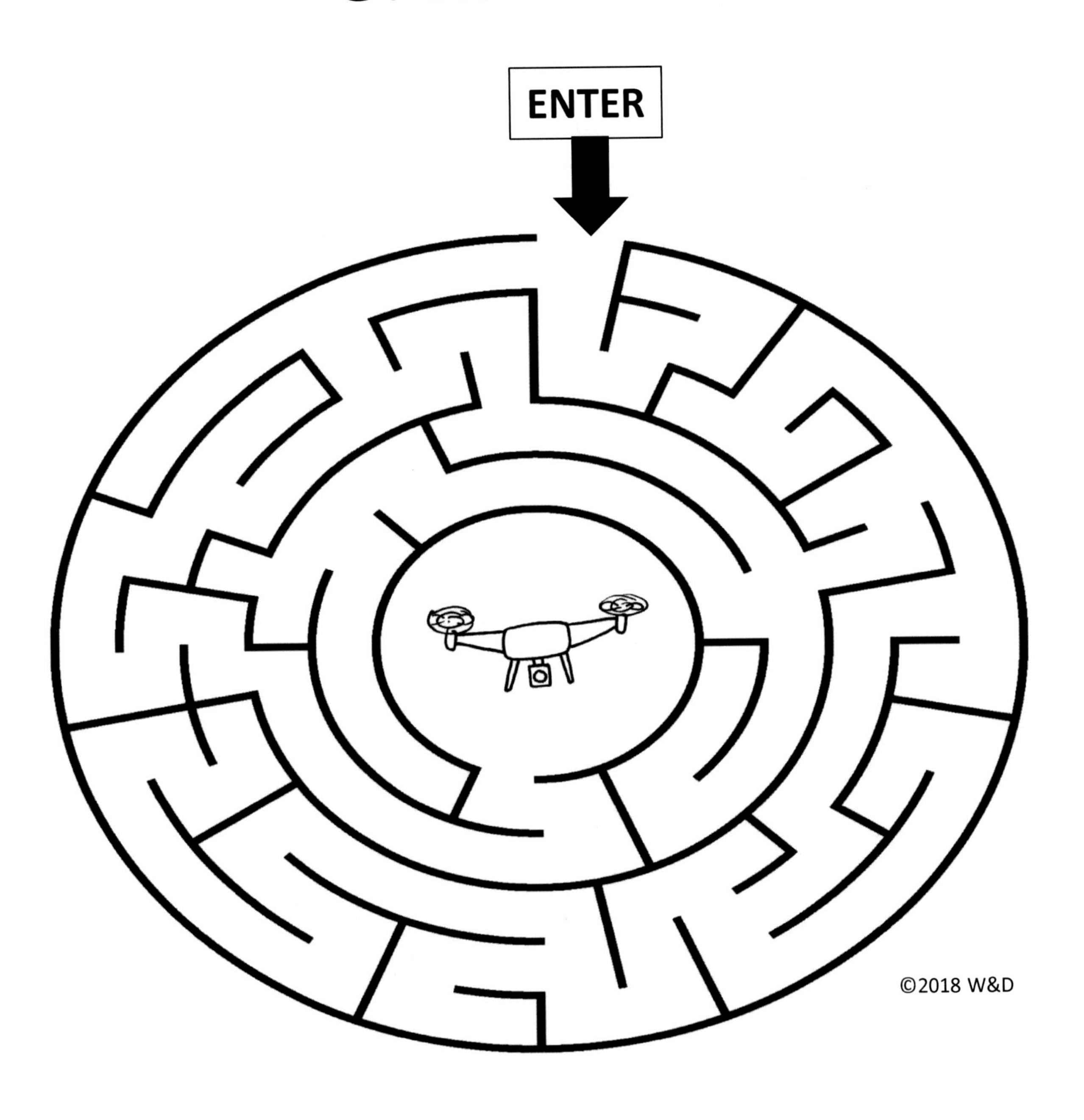

Find your way through the maze to find the drone.

Flying my drone with friends is fun!

Drones can be used to help design buildings.

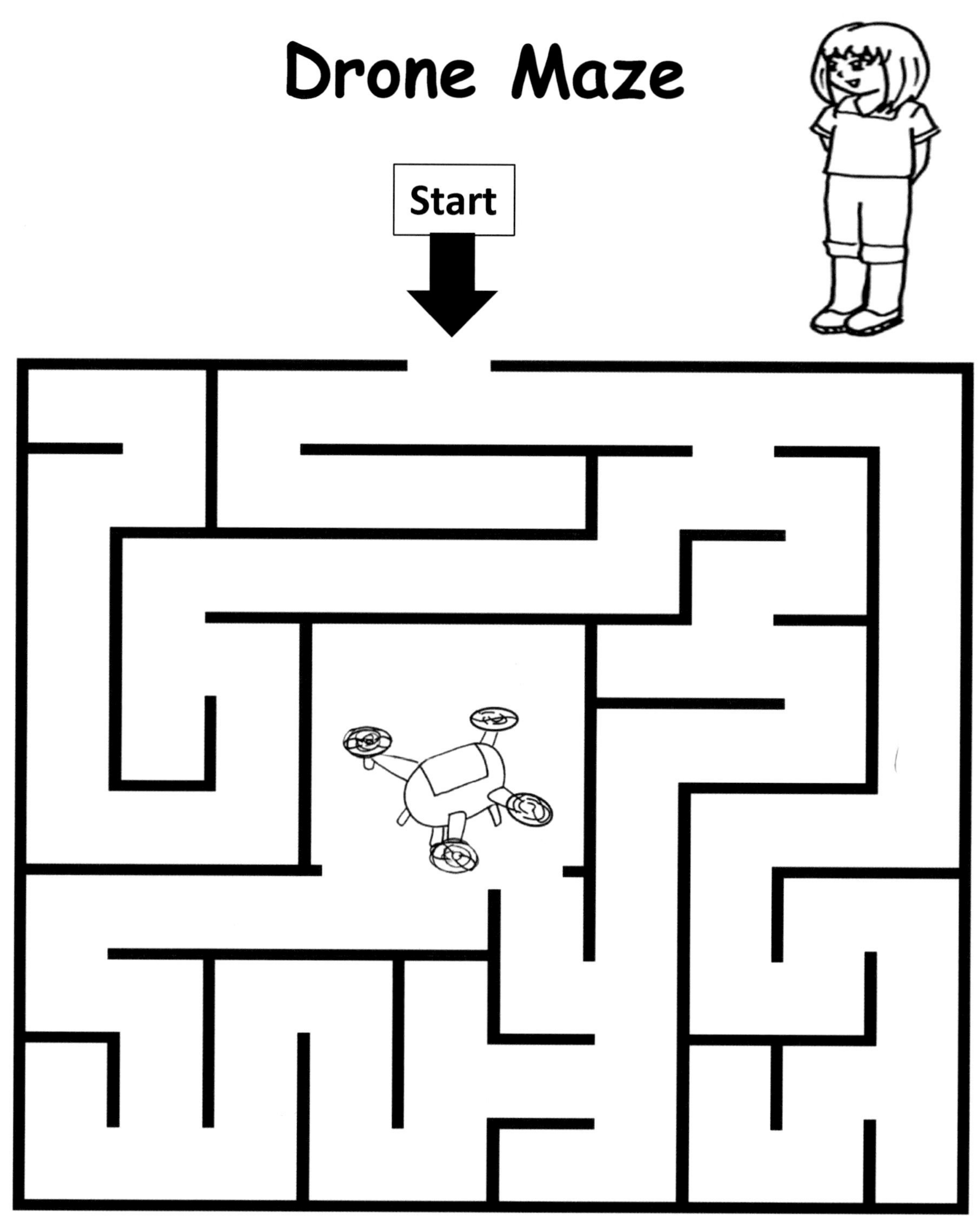

Help Olivia find her drone.

©2018 W&D
What's the difference?

What's the difference?

Drones can help save lives. What do you think is happening in this picture?

Many drones fly in the air but did you know some drones swim under water?

What's the difference?

What's the difference?

Criss Cross Puzzle

Write the word for each clue in the grid.

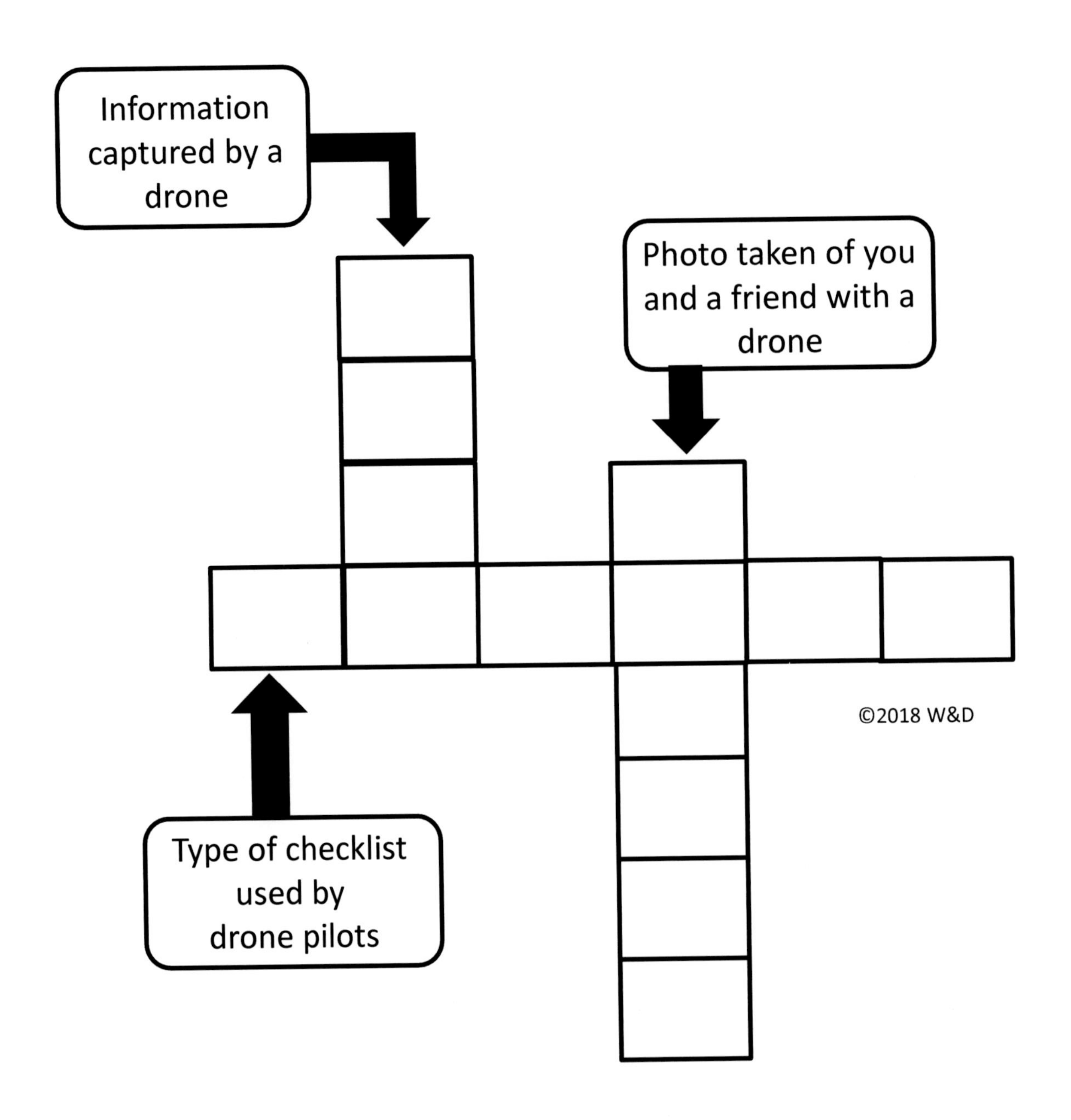

The best time to fly a drone is during the day when there is no rain or wind.

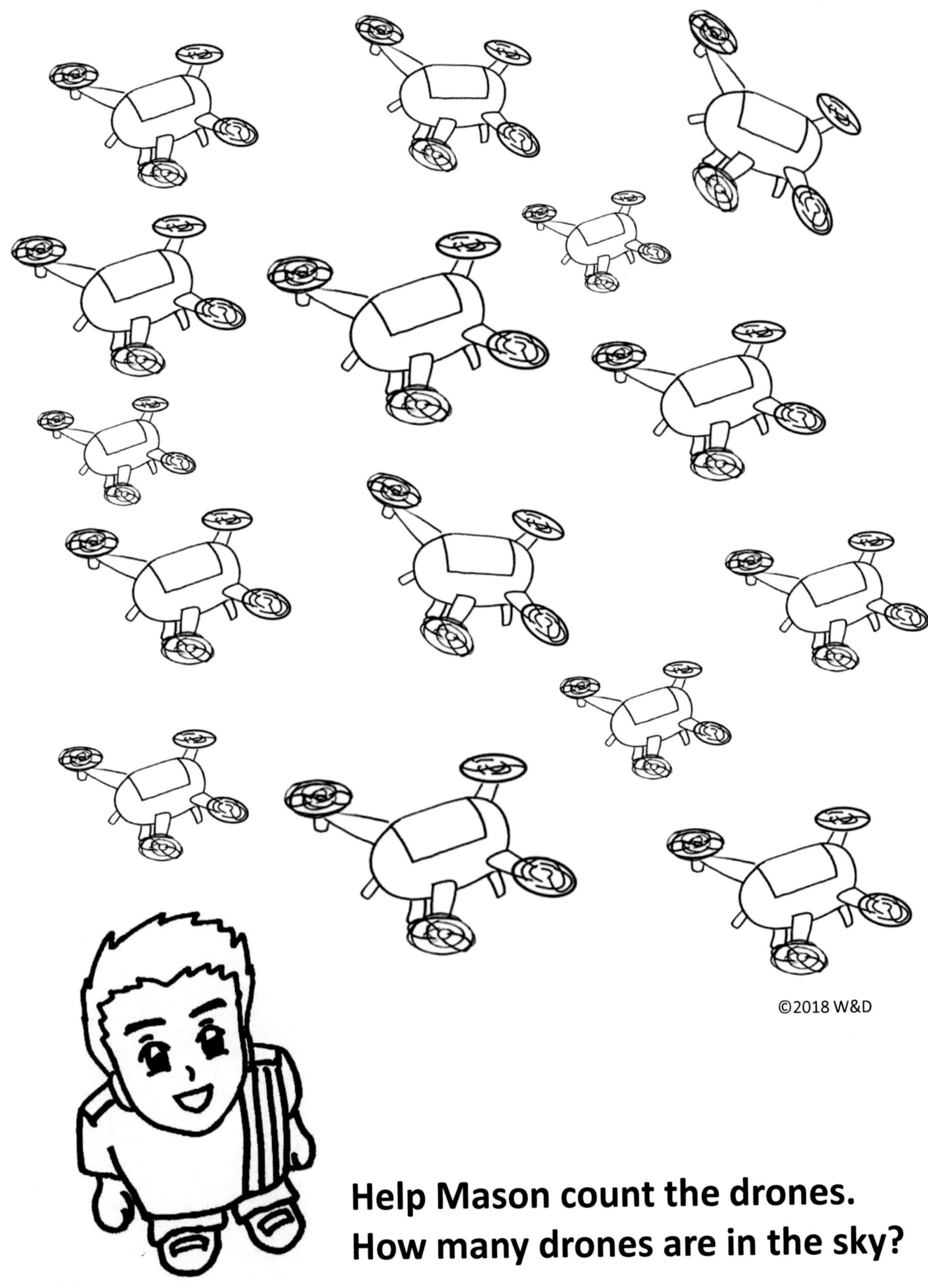

Help Mason count the drones.
How many drones are in the sky?

A friend can help you watch to make sure you are not flying your drone close to trees, wires or other drones.

Taking a drone training class is a smart way to learn how to safely fly a drone.

Made in the USA
Middletown, DE
18 August 2019